Pokémon™

FAMOUS FRIENDS & FOES

BY
RACHEL CHLEBOWSKI

A Random House PICTUREBACK® Book
Random House 🏠 New York

© 2017 The Pokémon Company International. © 1995–2017 Nintendo / Creatures Inc. / GAME FREAK inc.
TM, ®, and character names are trademarks of Nintendo. Published in the United States by Random House
Children's Books, a division of Penguin Random House LLC, 1745 Broadway, New York, NY 10019, and in
Canada by Penguin Random House Canada Limited, Toronto. Pictureback, Random House, and the
Random House colophon are registered trademarks of Penguin Random House LLC.
ISBN 978-1-5247-7010-5
randomhousekids.com
Printed in the United States of America
10 9 8 7 6 5

WELCOME TO THE WORLD OF **POKÉMON**!

Pokémon Trainers can catch these incredible creatures in the wild and Train them in battle to be the very best. Trainers just starting out in the Kanto region are likely to meet one of these three Pokémon early in their journey:

BULBASAUR is a Grass and Poison type with a seed on its back. While it naps in the sun, its seed absorbs sunlight and grows.

BULBASAUR
Category: Seed Pokémon
Height: 2'04" / **Weight:** 15.2 lbs.
Type: Grass-Poison

SQUIRTLE's shell protects it in battle. Its round shape and grooved surface allow the Pokémon to swim fast!

CHARMANDER is a Fire-type Pokémon. The flame on the tip of its tail indicates how it is feeling—if it flares up in a fury, watch out!

CHARMANDER
Category: Lizard Pokémon
Height: 2'00" / **Weight:** 18.7 lbs.
Type: Fire

SQUIRTLE
Category: Tiny Turtle Pokémon
Height: 1'08" / **Weight:** 19.8 lbs.
Type: Water

Some Pokémon can evolve into entirely different Pokémon. A variety of causes can lead to a Pokémon's Evolution.

When **BULBASAUR** evolves into **IVYSAUR**, the seed turns into a bud on Ivysaur's back. Ivysaur has stronger legs to support the bud's weight.

IVYSAUR
Category: Seed Pokémon
Height: 3'03" / **Weight:** 28.7 lbs.
Type: Grass-Poison

CHARMANDER evolves into **CHARMELEON**. When it becomes aggressive against a foe, the flame at the end of its tail turns bluish white.

CHARMELEON
Category: Flame Pokémon
Height: 3'07" / **Weight:** 41.9 lbs.
Type: Fire

WARTORTLE is the evolved form of **SQUIRTLE**. Wartortle's tail is large and covered with thick fur that darkens in color as it gets older.

WARTORTLE
Category: Turtle Pokémon
Height: 3'03" / **Weight:** 49.6 lbs.
Type: Water

IVYSAUR evolves into **VENUSAUR**. The large flower on its back is said to take on rich colors if it gets plenty of sunlight. It also has a soothing aroma.

VENUSAUR
Category: Seed Pokémon
Height: 6'07" / **Weight:** 220.5 lbs.
Type: Grass-Poison

When **CHARMELEON** evolves into **CHARIZARD**, it seeks out worthy opponents and only breathes fire against these stronger foes.

CHARIZARD
Category: Flame Pokémon
Height: 5'07" / **Weight:** 199.5 lbs.
Type: Fire-Flying

WARTORTLE evolves into **BLASTOISE**. The water spouts sticking out of its shell can hit their target from amazing distances!

BLASTOISE
Category: Shellfish Pokémon
Height: 5'03" / **Weight:** 188.5 lbs.
Type: Water

JIGGLYPUFF can inflate its body like a balloon and sing at the right wavelength to make its opponent fall asleep. It can keep singing until everyone listening falls asleep.

JIGGLYPUFF
Category: Balloon Pokémon
Height: 1'08" / Weight: 12.1 lbs.
Type: Normal-Fairy

DITTO is the Transform Pokémon. It can change its shape to resemble almost anything! It often uses this skill to try to befriend other Pokémon.

DITTO
Category: Transform Pokémon
Height: 1'00" / **Weight:** 8.8 lbs.
Type: Normal

DITTO PIKACHU
Category: Transform Pokémon
Height: 1'04" / **Weight:** 13.2 lbs.
Type: Electric

PIKACHU is an Electric-type Pokémon that stores electricity in its body. It releases that energy regularly to maintain good health.

PIKACHU
Category: Mouse Pokémon
Height: 1'04" / **Weight:** 13.2 lbs.
Type: Electric

PIKACHU evolves into **RAICHU**. This Pokémon can unleash so much electricity that it can defeat a much larger foe with a single shock!

RAICHU
Category: Mouse Pokémon
Height: 2'07" / Weight: 66.1 lbs.
Type: Electric

ALOLAN RAICHU
Category: Mouse Pokémon
Height: 2'04" / Weight: 46.3 lbs.
Type: Electric-Psychic

In the Alola region, **PIKACHU** evolves into **ALOLAN RAICHU**. Raichu is thought to look different in Alola because of what it eats. Alolan Raichu can use its psychic power to surf on its tail.

CLEFFA
Category: Star Shape Pokémon
Height: 1'00" / **Weight:** 6.6 lbs.
Type: Fairy

The Pokémon **CLEFFA**, first found in the Johto region, evolves into **CLEFAIRY**.

CLEFAIRY

Category: Fairy Pokémon
Height: 2'00" / **Weight:** 16.5 lbs.
Type: Fairy

Everyone loves **CLEFAIRY**! This Pokémon is charming but hard to find. When it dances under the full moon, a strange, compelling energy surrounds the area.

CLEFABLE

Category: Fairy Pokémon
Height: 4'03" / **Weight:** 88.2 lbs.
Type: Fairy

CLEFABLE is the evolved form of **CLEFAIRY**. Clefable usually live hidden far from people. But if you see two Clefable skipping along together, tradition says that you will have a happy marriage.

VULPIX is a Fire-type Pokémon that is beloved for its fur and its multiple tails, which keep splitting as it grows.

VULPIX
Category: Fox Pokémon
Height: 2'00" / Weight: 21.8 lbs.
Type: Fire

In Alola, **VULPIX** is an Ice-type Pokémon. If it gets too hot, its six tails can create a spray of ice crystals to cool itself off.

ALOLAN VULPIX
Category: Fox Pokémon
Height: 2'00" / Weight: 21.8 lbs.
Type: Ice

ALOLAN NINETALES

Category: Fox Pokémon
Height: 3'07" / **Weight:** 43.9 lbs.
Type: Ice-Fairy

NINETALES also has a different form in Alola, that of an Ice- and Fairy-type Pokémon. It is usually gentle, but when angered, it can freeze its enemies in their tracks.

VULPIX evolves into **NINETALES**. This Pokémon can live for a thousand years. According to myth, it was created when nine saints merged into a single being.

NINETALES

Category: Fox Pokémon
Height: 3'07" / **Weight:** 43.9 lbs.
Type: Fire

ZUBAT spends its days sleeping in caves and uses ultrasonic waves to sense its environment.

ZUBAT
Category: Bat Pokémon
Height: 2'07" / **Weight:** 16.5 lbs.
Type: Poison-Flying

When **ZUBAT** evolves into **GOLBAT**, it develops eyes to see with. It uses its hollow fangs to suck blood, but sometimes it eats so much that it can't fly afterward!

GOLBAT
Category: Bat Pokémon
Height: 5'03" / **Weight:** 121.3 lbs.
Type: Poison-Flying

CROBAT
Category: Bat Pokémon
Height: 5'11" / **Weight:** 165.3 lbs.
Type: Poison-Flying

CROBAT, the evolved form of **GOLBAT**, is a master of stealth and speed. Its hind legs have become an extra pair of wings!

MEOWTH has lazy days and active nights. It loves coins and shiny objects like the one on its head.

MEOWTH
Category: Scratch Cat Pokémon
Height: 1'04" / **Weight:** 9.3 lbs.
Type: Normal

ALOLAN MEOWTH
Category: Scratch Cat Pokémon
Height: 1'04" / **Weight:** 9.3 lbs.
Type: Dark

In Alola, **MEOWTH** is a Dark-type Pokémon. It is very vain about the golden Charm on its forehead, and it grows enraged if the Charm gets dirty.

PSYDUCK
Category: Duck Pokémon
Height: 2'07" / Weight: 43.2 lbs.
Type: Water

PSYDUCK has mysterious psychic powers, but its terrible headaches make it too miserable to control these powers.

GASTLY's presence can cause lights to flicker in the abandoned buildings it likes to lurk in. Though it is hard to see, this Pokémon gives off a delicately sweet scent.

GASTLY
Category: Gas Pokémon
Height: 4'03" / **Weight:** 0.2 lbs.
Type: Ghost-Poison

GASTLY evolves into **HAUNTER**. Haunter's lick can steal your life energy! It prefers to live in darkness and avoids city lights.

HAUNTER
Category: Gas Pokémon
Height: 5'03" / **Weight:** 0.2 lbs.
Type: Ghost-Poison

GENGAR is the evolved form of **HAUNTER**. When Gengar approaches, it brings an unexplainable chill to the air. Its mixed-up idea of friendship has led it to attack humans in an attempt to become friends.

GENGAR
Category: Shadow Pokémon
Height: 4'11" / **Weight:** 89.3 lbs.
Type: Ghost-Poison

CUBONE

Category: Lonely Pokémon
Height: 1'04" / **Weight:** 14.3 lbs.
Type: Ground

CUBONE is the Lonely Pokémon. It weeps for its lost mother, leaving tearstains on the skull it wears. Some think that learning to cope with its grief is the only way Cubone can evolve.

MAROWAK, CUBONE's evolved form, is a fearsome foe that uses bones as weapons against those it considers enemies.

MAROWAK
Category: Bone Keeper Pokémon
Height: 3'03" / **Weight:** 99.2 lbs.
Type: Ground

ALOLAN MAROWAK
Category: Bone Keeper Pokémon
Height: 3'03" / **Weight:** 75.0 lbs.
Type: Fire-Ghost

ALOLAN MAROWAK is unlike **MAROWAK** seen in other regions. The flaming bone it uses to defend itself once belonged to its mother, and its mother's spirit protects it.

MAGIKARP

Category: Fish Pokémon
Height: 2'11" / **Weight:** 22.0 lbs.
Type: Water

MAGIKARP's habit of splashing about recklessly leaves it open to attack. Though it's not the strongest fighter in battle, it does exist in huge numbers.

When **MAGIKARP** evolves into **GYARADOS**, it grows about ten times larger! Gyarados has a notorious temper and aptitude for destruction.

GYARADOS
Category: Atrocious Pokémon
Height: 21'04" / **Weight:** 518.1 lbs.
Type: Water-Flying

LAPRAS

Category: Transport Pokémon
Height: 8'02" / **Weight:** 485.0 lbs.
Type: Water-Ice

LAPRAS has a lovely singing voice. Friendly and intelligent, this Pokémon is often used for transportation on water.

SNORLAX

Category: Sleeping Pokémon
Height: 6'11" / **Weight:** 1014.1 lbs.
Type: Normal

SNORLAX's massive body needs about 900 pounds of food every day. It can eat just about anything! If it falls asleep while eating, it will continue to eat in its sleep.

EEVEE is the Evolution Pokémon. Its unstable genetic structure enables it to evolve into eight different Pokémon, according to current studies.

EEVEE • **Category:** Evolution Pokémon
Height: 1'00" / **Weight:** 14.3 lbs. **Type:** Normal

VAPOREON • **Category:** Bubble Jet Pokémon
Height: 3'03" / **Weight:** 63.9 lbs. **Type:** Water

JOLTEON • **Category:** Lightning Pokémon
Height: 2'07" / **Weight:** 54.0 lbs. **Type:** Electric

FLAREON • **Category:** Flame Pokémon
Height: 2'11" / **Weight:** 55.1 lbs. **Type:** Fire

ESPEON • **Category:** Sun Pokémon
Height: 2'11" / **Weight:** 58.4 lbs. **Type:** Psychic

GLACEON • **Category:** Fresh Snow Pokémon
Height: 2'07" / **Weight:** 57.1 lbs. **Type:** Ice

LEAFEON • **Category:** Verdant Pokémon
Height: 3'03" / **Weight:** 56.2 lbs. **Type:** Grass

SYLVEON • **Category:** Intertwining Pokémon
Height: 3'03" / **Weight:** 51.8 lbs. **Type:** Fairy

UMBREON • **Category:** Moonlight Pokémon
Height: 3'03" / **Weight:** 59.5 lbs. **Type:** Dark

DRATINI was thought to be mere rumor, until a fisherman caught one after battling it for many hours. Its skin, which it sheds often as it grows, is sometimes used to make clothing.

DRATINI
Category: Dragon Pokémon
Height: 5'11" / **Weight:** 7.3 lbs.
Type: Dragon

DRATINI evolves into **DRAGONAIR**, a Pokémon respected by farmers due to its fabled ability to change the weather with the crystalline orbs on its body.

DRAGONAIR
Category: Dragon Pokémon
Height: 13'01" / **Weight:** 36.4 lbs.
Type: Dragon

DRAGONITE evolves from **DRAGONAIR**.
Dragonite's wrath can be devastating.
Luckily, this Pokémon has a kind
and calm demeanor and is
slow to anger.

DRAGONITE
Category: Dragon Pokémon
Height: 7'03" / **Weight:** 463.0 lbs.
Type: Dragon-Flying

MEW
Category: New Species Pokémon
Height: 1'04" / **Weight:** 8.8 lbs.
Type: Psychic

MEW is said to possess the genetic makeup of all Pokémon. It can make itself invisible so that people will not notice it!

MEWTWO was created by genetic manipulation in an effort to re-create **MEW**. While this Pokémon is strong in both mind and body, it's made most dangerous by its lack of compassion.

MEWTWO
Category: Genetic Pokémon
Height: 6'07" / **Weight:** 269.0 lbs.
Type: Psychic

The Pokémon world is an exciting place full of incredible, beloved Pokémon for you to discover. Train your Pokémon well as your journey continues!